THE GOLDEN EGG
A COMIC ADVENTURE

WRITTEN AND ILLUSTRATED
BY
MIMI BRENNAN

Holiday House   New York

To my dear Mother and to all those who believed in this book.

☆ CONTENTS ☆

Printed in the United States of America
First Edition

Library of Congress Cataloging-in-Publication Data

Brennan, Mimi.
The golden egg : a comic adventure / written and illustrated by
Mimi Brennan. — 1st ed.
p.   cm.
Summary: Martin Mallard fights back when evil Alfred Duckmuck
frames him for the theft of a golden egg and endangers the lives of
the wild ducks living outside of Duckville.
ISBN 0-8234-0796-9
[1. Ducks—Fiction.] I. Title.
PZ7.B75163Go   1990
[E]—dc20   89-20050   CIP   AC
ISBN 0-8234-0796-9

THE MAIN CHARACTERS

MARTIN MALLARD

A newspaper reporter accused of a crime he didn't commit

ALFRED DUCKMUCK

A rotten duck who will do anything for money

CLARENCE QUACKENBUSH

Martin Mallard's friend and lawyer

SERGEANT QUACKERS

A police Sergeant who finds the golden egg

T.E. BEARHART

An artist who rescues Martin Mallard from near-death

SWANEE SWANSON

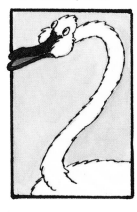

A wild Swan who teaches Martin Mallard to fly

JEFFREY WOLF

A mysterious wolf whom Martin Mallard meets one night

ORVILLE McKEEVER

BILLY-JOE McKEEVER

BOBBY-SAM McKEEVER

Three duck hunters who are Alfred Duckmuck's business partners

① Hidden deep in the cattails of The Great Wild Marsh is the tiny town of Duckville.

Gold Pond

The Great Wild Marsh

Goose Island

Quackertown ☆ Duckville

Silver Lake

Swan Lake

The Magnificent Forest

Beastietown ☆

② All the wild ducks, geese and swans live in the Great Wild Marsh outside of Duckville.

③ All the domestic ducks live in Duckville. They have forgotten how to fly. Duckville's a friendly town and a safe place to raise ducklings.

I wouldn't live anywhere else!

Welcome to Duckville!

④ But the wild ducks outside of Duckville aren't safe. From late fall until early winter, they fear the hunter's gun. The hunters eat only wild ducks because they taste better.

Fly fast or we'll be duck soup tonight!

⑤ The unlucky duckies end up as:

DUCK STEW WITH WILD RICE

DUCK POT PIE

ROAST DUCK

⑥ Some domestic ducks are concerned about all the duck hunts in The Great Wild Marsh. They protest to show their sympathy for the wild ducks.

THE DAILY QUACK

ALFRED DUCKMUCK DONATES

Duckmuck Makes Big Donation to Duckville Orphanage

HUMPHREY DUCKFAT WINS PIE-EATING CONTEST

THE DAILY QUACK

october 26

HUNTING SEASON OPENS, DOMESTIC DUCKS PROTEST!

It's Hunting season: Do you know where your Lil' ducky is?

STOP THE DUCK HUNTS NOW!

⑦ Martin Mallard, a reporter for <u>The Daily Quack</u> in Duckville, had been writing articles against the duck hunts.

Boss, I have a great story!

What's the scoop, Martin?

⑧ A wild duck told me that some duck is pretending to be a wild duck to attract wild ducks for the hunters!

And who is this rotten duck?

⑨ Nobody knows. Let me hang out in the marsh and see what I can find out.

That would be very dangerous! You could get your tailfeathers blown off!

⑩ I'll be all right! Don't I always get my story?

Sure! You're my best reporter. Just be careful!

⑪ That night, after interviewing some wild ducks, Martin took a walk in the marsh.

A beautiful night...

⑫ Then, as he passed the hunter's lodge, he bumped into Alfred Duckmuck, an important Duckville citizen.

What's Duckmuck doing so near the hunter's lodge?

It's that nosy Martin Mallard from The Daily Quack.

13 Alfred Duckmuck! What brings you out here?

Just taking a walk, and you?

14 I've been interviewing wild ducks for my next article.

Your articles about the duck hunts are upsetting everyone in Duckville!

15 Some duck is a decoy for the hunters. I've got to find out who it is.

Be careful! Your curiosity may get you in trouble! Curiosity killed the cat...

16 Or is it the duck? Ha! Ha! Yuk! Yuk!

Very funny, Mr. Duckmuck, very funny!

17 Yet, despite their differences, the two ducks parted in a friendly way.

Well, good-bye Martin Mallard. I just wanted to give you a little advice.

Thanks, but too many wild ducks have been shot. I've got to find that decoy!

18 If he finds out about me, I'll be a stuck duck! I've got to do something about him... quick!

19 I think Duckmuck's hiding something.

20

I'm going to find out what it is!

The Duckville Inn

21 That night, before Martin went to sleep, he thought of a plan.

Tomorrow night I'll hide near the hunters' lodge.

22 Meanwhile, out in the marsh, Duckmuck visited the McKeever brothers.

What took you so long?

Orville, I met this nosy duck. I'm afraid he might find out about us.

23 Several weeks before, Duckmuck had agreed to be their decoy.

How would you like to help us trap wild ducks? We'll pay you lots of money.

Sure I'll help you. The only good wild duck is a dead one! Ha! Ha!

24 He pretended he was a wild duck to attract the wild ducks for the McKeevers to shoot.

Keep waving to them, Duckmuck.

Hurry up and shoot! I'm freezing!

25 He also told them where to find the wild ducks. He had been spying on them for weeks.

Where are those ducks?

26 The McKeevers paid him in teeny tiny gold bits.

Here's for being such a good decoy.

You're going to be a rich duck.

He already is a rich duck, you pinhead!

Thanks!

27 Duckmuck was already rich from making duckweed into a fast food, but he wanted to be even richer.

DUCKMUCK'S DUCKWEED BREAD

Yummy!

DUCKMUCK'S DUCKWEED PIE

Yum Yum!

DUCKMUCK'S DUCKWEED COOKIES

So Yummy!

Yum!

DUCKMUCK'S DUCKWEED SODA

28 He loved money more than anything in the world.

That duck will do anything for money.

I wouldn't want to be his enemy.

29 Duckmuck hoped he might be given more gold for warning the McKeevers about Martin.

We'll watch out for that Snoopy Martin Mallard.

You better be a good lil' ducky! Ha! Ha!

I'll be good as gold. Hee! Hee!

30 From the gold the hunters gave him, Duckmuck made a beautiful egg.

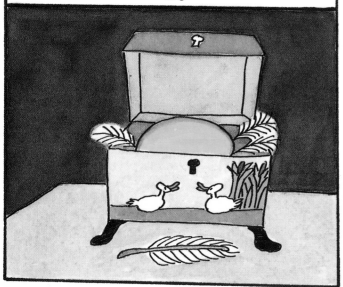

31 He thought the egg was magic. He often talked to it, hoping it would bring him good luck.

Egg, tell me what to do about Martin Mallard.

32 That night, Duckmuck went to sleep with the egg under his pillow. A plan for getting rid of Martin came to him in a dream.

③③ The next night, Duckmuck put the golden egg in a basket and went to Martin Mallard's house.

I hope he's going out.

③④ Finally, Martin left to take a walk to Silver Lake.

It's about time!

③⑤ Duckmuck opened the door...

③⑥ And looked for a place to hide the egg.

Perfect!

③⑦ Then he went home.

What a clever old duck I am! Hee! Hee!

③⑧ The next morning, Duckmuck put the next part of his plan into action. He told the police that his egg had been stolen.

Don't worry. Sergeant Quackers and I will search all the houses in Duckville.

③⑨ After the police searched most of the houses, they came to Martin Mallard's.

We're almost done, Martin. Sorry to bother you.

It's ok, Chief. How about some tea?

Oh no... Chief!

40 What is it, Quackers?

Chief... it's Duckmuck's golden egg!

41 Martin, why did you steal this egg?

I didn't steal it! I swear it!

42 There were more questions.

But why was the egg in your chest?

I don't know! Maybe Duckmuck put it there!

Be careful! Mr. Duckmuck is one of our best citizens!

43 Martin... We'll have to take you to the jail.

Listen, Chief, I didn't steal that egg!

44 You have to go to jail 'til your trial. That's the law! Quackers, tell him his rights.

I am an innocent duck!

You have the right to remain silent. Anything you say or do can be used against you. If you do not have a lawyer, the court will appoint one.

45 They went on their way to jail.

This can't be true.

Sometimes I hate my job.

(46) At the Duckville jail, Martin was given a prison uniform. A sketch was done for the police record book.

Name: Johnny Duckrot
Bramble Bush Rd.
Quackertown
Occupation: Bum
Crime: Stealing little ducklings.

Name: Martin Mallard
6 Cattail Lane
Duckville
Occupation: Newspaper reporter
Crime: Stealing Alfred Duckmuck's golden egg.

(47) Then they put Martin in a dark, damp cell.

What am I doing here?

(48) His friend and lawyer Clarence Quackenbush visited.

This is going to be a hard case to win. The judge is a good friend of Duckmuck's.

It's hopeless.

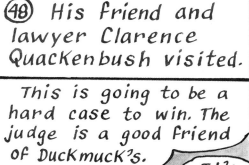

(49) Nothing is hopeless! I'll do everything I can for you. We'll fight!

Thanks, Clarence.

(50) Martin's friends believed in his innocence. Martin had lived in Duckville for only a few years. He didn't have as many friends as Duckmuck.

Duckmuck, on the other hand, was a very popular duck. It would be hard for Martin to prove that Duckmuck was guilty.

THE DAILY QUACK

IS THIS THE FACE OF A THIEF?

The staff of this paper support Martin Mallard. "He didn't want riches," said his editor Max Ducker, "all he wanted was to write the truth."

THE DAI

November 6

DUCKMUCK NAMED AS "DUCK OF THE YEAR"

"No other duck has given more to Duckville,"

(51) Clarence Quackenbush couldn't convince the judge to delay the trial.

We need more time to get solid evidence against Duckmuck.

(52) At Martin's trial, the cards were stacked against him. He had no witnesses to testify that he was out in the marsh on the night Duckmuck's egg was stolen.

Martin Mallard stole Duckmuck's golden egg!

Anyone with a heart can see he is innocent!

(53) Finally, the dreaded moment came.

This court has found you guilty. Your punishment is three years in the Duckville jail.

Oh no. No!

(54) Sergeant Quackers took Martin back to jail.

We won't give up! I'll prove your innocence!

(55) Weeks passed and Martin was miserable.

I can't stand this awful loneliness.

(56) Clarence was having a hard time finding evidence against Duckmuck.

Hunting season's almost over. Every night for the last two weeks I've been out at the hunting lodge. No one's been there. It's going to be a long time 'til we find anything against Duckmuck.

Sigh...

57 They won't let me read or write anything. I'm going crazy. I must do something!

58 The only good thing about jail was playing cards with Sergeant Quackers.

I've got you now, Martin!

Ha! Just wait 'til you see my card.

59 Martin sensed that Quackers liked him.

If you don't eat, you'll get sick.

I've got to get out of here.

60 One night, Quackers was the only guard in the jail. Martin had an idea.

Auugh! I have a burning pain around my waist.

It sounds like your appendix.

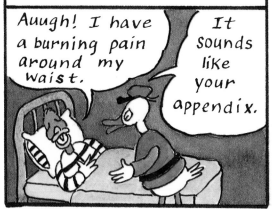

61 We better get you to the doctor. Can you walk?

Gasp! Gasp! I think so.

62 Hold on to my arm.

63 Suddenly, Martin turned around and socked Quackers hard on the head. He took Quackers' keys and locked him in the cell.

Sorry, Quackers, but I had to do this!

64 Quickly, he ran home and packed his carpet bag. Then, he was on his way.

Good-bye little town that I love...

65 Martin walked through the marsh heading South. He was so happy to be free!

When they find out I'm gone, it will be morning. They'll never find me.

66 He decided to go through The Magnificent Forest to Beastie town.

The Great Wild Marsh

The Magnificent Forest

Beastie town ☆

Goose Is.

67 It was mid-November. Food was scarce. Since Martin couldn't fly, he had to walk.

It's lonely out here. Everyone's gone south.

68 One night he shared a meal with a wild duck couple. They gave him some good advice about facing life's troubles.

During hunting season, fly high, fly strong and fly fast; else they'll shoot you in the tailfeathers.

69 After two weeks, Martin came to The Magnificent Forest. He was very hungry, cold and tired.

Some say there are wolves in these woods.

70 Whatever happens, I'll be all right. I'll be all right...

71. A week passed, and Martin saw no one. Most animals were asleep for the winter. One night, he hid from some thieves.

Please... don't come this way.

But I heard a noise behind them trees, Redd!

Listen, Rocky, we've got to get away before the cops come.

72. A few nights later, while eating some berries, Martin felt someone was behind him. He was afraid to turn around.

73. Slowly, he turned around...

YIKES! A WOLF!

Hullo, I'm Jeffrey Wolf. Who are you?

74.

I'm Ma... Ma... Martin Mal... Mallard.

Nice to meet you, Mr. Mallard. Don't be scared. I won't hurt you.

75. The wolf asked the duck where he was going. He offered the hospitality of his den, but Martin said he was in a hurry to get to Beastietown.

I'm not like other wolves. I eat only vegetables. You need good food and a warm place.

He seems so nice... but look what happened to poor Little Red Riding Hood...

76.

If you come back, my den is two trees to the left.

I'm sick of trying to prove I'm not a bad guy.

I'm so cold and hungry, but it's too risky.

Thanks.

17

⑦ For the next two days, it snowed. Martin was feeling very strange. First he felt hot, then he had cold chills.

⑦⑧ The more he walked, the dizzier he felt. His head ached and his eyes hurt.

If I fall asleep, I'll freeze to death. I've got to get up.

⑦⑨ He walked a little further. He saw a light in the distance.

⑧⓪ He went toward the light until he found himself in front of a tree house.

They look friendly. I'll ask if I can stay a few nights. I'll do chores to earn my keep.

⑧① He knocked but had no strength. His knock was too soft to hear.

⑧② Suddenly, everything spun around him. Darkness came over his eyes. He took a deep breath and collapsed.

83) Inside, T.E. Bearhart was having tea with Bernie Big Ears, his neighbor. Suddenly, he saw something at the window.

Bernie, there's something outside. Look!

Bearhart, I don't see anything but wind and snow.

84) Something's out there. I'm going outside!

Bearhart, don't go! Maybe it's a mean animal. You'll get hurt!

85) I'm not scared. I've got to see what's out there.

Bearhart, wait!

86)

87) He feels so cold. Is he still alive?

Yes, but his pulse is weak. We've got to get him warm.

88) How's his pulse?

Much better, but he might have pneumonia. Let's put him to bed.

(89) The rabbit knew a lot about medicine. He gave Martin some penicillin he had made from bread mold. All night, Bearhart and Bernie stayed by Martin's bedside.

His temperature is 103°. I'm afraid we'll lose him if his fever doesn't break.

(90) In the middle of the night, Martin had a bad dream. His temperature was 104°.

I didn't do it! I'm innocent!

(91) In his next dream, he saw the most beautiful egg. There was a warm, glowy light coming from it. Never in his life had he seen anything more wonderful.
   Slowly, the egg floated toward him. He reached out to touch it, but it vanished.

(92) By the next morning, Martin's fever had broken. He awoke to see two strange animals looking down at him.

Where am... I?

You're with friends. You had a fever. We almost lost you. You're going to be fine.

CHAPTER 5
NEW FRIENDS

93) As each day passed, Martin grew stronger. One night he told Bearhart all about Duckmuck and jail.

94) Bearhart told Martin that he could stay with him as long as he wished. Life with the bear was fun and never dull.

Bearhart, what are you doing?

Standing on my head.

95) Martin found a good job as a reporter for The Beastietown Times. Bearhart made a fine living as a portrait painter.

You have wonderful eyes... like two perfect fried eggs.

96) Through Bearhart, Martin met some very nice animals, including Jeffrey Wolf, who was one of Bearhart's good friends.

I'm sorry I acted like a silly goose the night I met you.

Don't worry about it. I understand.

(97) One of Martin's favorite things was going to the Beastietown market every other week to buy food.

(98) One day at the market, Madame Zena told them their fortunes.

You must prove you are innocent of a crime.

How could she know I want to go back to Duckville to clear my name?

You do?

(99) That night, Martin came up with a plan for going back to Duckville.

I'll disguise myself as a wild duck. I'll have to learn to fly.

My friend Swanee Swanson can teach you.

(100) But... you'll be there during hunting season. You might get shot! Oh, I don't know if this is a good idea.

Don't worry. I just won't fly when the hunters are around. I'll trust my instincts, my deepest feelings.

(101) But wild ducks trust their instincts, and they still get shot.

Then they don't trust themselves enough. They let their fear get in the way.

102 Bearhart decided that he would go with Martin to Duckville, since he was worried that something bad might happen to the duck.

I'll pretend I'm doing a travel story on Duckville. I'll stay with your friend Clarence Quackenbush.

The Beastietown Times

I'll write and ask Clarence if that's O.K.

103 Finally, Martin met the remarkable Swanee Swanson.

You have excellent wings for a domestic duck, but you'll have to exercise to strengthen them.

104 Everyday for two hours, Martin did wing exercises. Bearhart and Bernie played music to make it easier.

Puff! Puff!

105 And every night ...

Oooh, I ache and ache. This is harder than I thought.

106 When Martin's wings were strong, Swanee put him on a flying machine.

107 Next, Martin put on a glider. He took off from the highest hill in the meadow.

23

108 Finally, he was ready to fly on his own. First, he got a running start.

This is it!!

109 He lifted off,

110 and went up,

111 then, quickly down.

112 Swanee took him aside and gave him a little pep talk.

You lost control because you were scared. Let go of your fear and trust yourself. Believe in yourself, and you will fly!

113 I'm going to do it. Nothing can stop me. I will fly!

114 And that's just what happened.

If everyone could fly, the world would be a better place.

CHAPTER 6
OFF TO DUCKVILLE

(115) In September, Bearhart received a letter from Clarence Quackenbush inviting him to be his guest in Duckville. Bearhart and Martin were to leave in October. Bearhart was going to travel on Swanee's back, and Martin was going to fly next to them.

Martin, don't fly when there are hunters around. Just before Duckville, we'll separate. I'll meet you later at Silver Lake.

All right Swanee. Bearhart, don't worry. You'll love flying.

(116) Martin was right. Bearhart discovered that flying was the best thing in the world.

After three days, the friends reached The Great Wild Marsh. Just before Duckville, they said good-bye to Martin.

(117) Bearhart and Swanee flew to the edge of town where Clarence Quackenbush and his family were waiting.

THE DUCK HOUSE DINER

118 After Swanee left to meet Martin on Silver Lake, Bearhart and Clarence went for a walk.

What's Martin up to? I know he's up to something.

He doesn't have a plan. He and Swanee will stay with the wild ducks and try to catch that rotten duck who's helping the hunters.

119 The next afternoon Alfred Duckmuck invited Bearhart to lunch at his big mansion.

Why did you come to Duckville during hunting season? It's the worst time of year to visit.

Oops! I'd better have a good answer.

120 Well... um, because Duckville is the most beautiful at this time of year.

I'd better keep an eye on him.

121 Early the next morning on Silver Lake, a wild hen swam up to Martin.

Some duck found a big bunch of juicy snails! Hurry!

Snails? Yuck! I'd better go and pretend I'm excited.

(122) Martin didn't wake Swanee because the swan didn't like to eat snails. As Martin swam up to the other ducks, he saw someone who looked very familiar.

Oh no! It's DUCKMUCK!

And I saw more snails over there.

(123)

EVERYBODY! FLY! He's a decoy for the hunters! The hunters must be hiding nearby!

(124) Martin was so angry that he began to chase Duckmuck. Duckmuck swam as fast as he could toward the hunters.

I'm going to get you, DUCKMUCK!

125. Then Duckmuck called out to the hunters.

Help!

126. A shot rang out and Martin went down into the water.

127. Lady, the McKeevers hunting dog, swam out to retrieve him.

128. Everything happened so fast. By the time Swanee realized where Martin was, it was too late.

He was the best duck I ever knew. How am I going to tell Bearhart about this?

That wild duck gave you a hard time. Ha! Ha!

It's not funny, Billy-Joe!

129. Swanee flew back to Duckville to tell Bearhart about Martin.

We've got to go to the marsh and nab Duckmuck before it's too late.

We've got to find Sergeant Quackers!

130. They convinced Sergeant Quackers to go with them.

131) They hid in the cattails until Duckmuck came back with the McKeever brothers.

132) Through the open window, they heard the McKeevers tell Duckmuck that they didn't need him as a decoy anymore. Duckmuck was furious.

Now don't be upset. We can't afford to pay you anymore. Instead, we'll be using this battery-operated duck decoy.

Just don't come crawling back to me when your stupid decoy falls apart!

Wow! It flaps its wings and it even Quacks!

And it doesn't throw temper tantrums like Duckmuck!

Quack! Quack!

(133) Billy-Joe was about to pluck Martin's feathers. He picked him up and showed him to Duckmuck.

If it wasn't for us, Duckmuck, this duck would have gotten you. Hmm... He feels warm.

(134) Suddenly, Martin jumped up and flew out of Billy-Joe's arms. Duckmuck was so scared that he quacked.

Quack!

I'm going to get you, DUCKMUCK!

(135) At that moment, the door burst open and in rushed Bearhart and his friends, who joined in the chase.

(136) It didn't take long to catch Duckmuck.

You're under arrest, Duckmuck!

But the hunters made me be a decoy! They said they'd shoot me if I didn't do it!

We were outside. We heard everything!

You'd say anything just to save your own tailfeathers, Duckmuck!

He told us that he hid his golden egg in Martin Mallard's house!

(137) Sergeant Quackers took Duckmuck away to jail.

(138) Martin showed everyone the bullet-proof vest with the fake blood that had saved his life.

The ducks around here are too smart. Let's hunt where there are just plain old ducks!

Yes! Ducks who only fly and quack!

139 Duckmuck confessed that he had hidden the golden egg in Martin Mallard's house. Everyone asked Martin's forgiveness. The mayor presented him with the golden egg at the Duckville Opera House.

Thank you! I'll sell this egg and use the money to fight against the duck hunts. The wild ducks need our help! Let's all work together to stop the hunters from hunting wild ducks!

HOORAY! We'll stop the duck hunts! HOORAY!

140 Duckmuck was sentenced to four years in jail. He had to listen to the sad stories of those wild ducks who had lost loved ones in the duck hunts.

My husband was killed in the duck hunts. You were the hunters' decoy. How could you do this to me? Sob!

141 Martin found it hard to say good-bye to his good friends Bearhart and Swanee.

I don't know how to thank you.

Just come visit us often!

142 Martin Mallard was very glad to be back in his little house in the cattails.

Hullo my home, sweet home!